Amelia's
MIDDLE SCHOOL SURVIVAL GUIDE

by Marissa Moss

(and tough survivalist Amelia)

FEATURING

Amelia's MOST UNFORGETTABLE EMBARRASSING MOMENTS

Amelia's Guide to Gossip

do this—
I know I
can!

SIMON & SCHUSTER BOOKS FOR YOUNG READERS

NEW YORK   LONDON   TORONTO   SYDNEY

This is how **I** survive middle school, by making notebooks!
↓

Amelia's Science Fair Disaster

Amelia's Guide to Babysitting

Amelia's Itchy-Twitchy, Lovey-Dovey Summer at Camp Mosquito

Vote 4 Amelia

Amelia's 7th-Grade Notebook

Amelia's Must-Keep Resolutions for the Best Year Ever!

Amelia's Guide to Gossip

Amelia's Longest, Biggest, Most-Fights-Ever Family Reunion

Amelia's Book of Notes & Note Passing

Amelia's Most Unforgettable Embarrassing Moments

Amelia's 6th-Grade Notebook

But first I had to survive elementary school with **these** notebooks!
↓

Amelia's Family Ties

Amelia Tells All

The All-New Amelia

Amelia's Are-We-There-Yet Longest Ever Car Trip

Amelia's School Survival Guide

Amelia's 5th-Grade Notebook

Amelia's Bully Survival Guide

Amelia Writes Again

Amelia's Boredom Survival Guide

Amelia's Notebook

My first notebook ever! ↗

↖ The one that started it all!

Amelia's MOST UNFORGETTABLE EMBARRASSING MOMENTS

by Marissa Moss
(except all embarrassment is entirely amelia's!)

TOP SECRET

Blush-ometer-
DANGER!! →
WAAAAY IN
THE RED ZONE!

Simon & Schuster Books for Young Readers
New York   London   Toronto   Sydney

CAUTION: CONTENTS UNDER PRESSURE! →

SAYING STUPID THINGS COULD BE HAZARDOUS TO YOUR HEALTH!

I thought being in middle school meant you were finally beyond stupid, embarrassing moments. Like you're smart enough NOT to think "adept" means "inept" (just the opposite!) or that the plural of "spaghetti" is "spaghettis" or that "potato" is spelled like it's part of a foot ("potatoe"). I thought at a certain age you outgrew that kind of dumbness, and stupid things didn't come out of your mouth anymore.

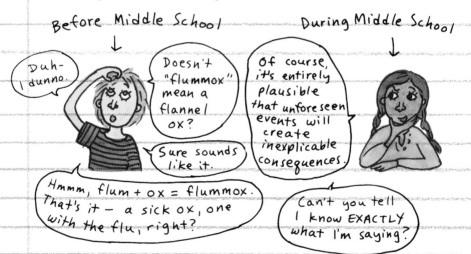

Before Middle School ↓

During Middle School ↓

Duh—I dunno.

Doesn't "flummox" mean a flannel ox?

Sure sounds like it.

Hmmm, flum + ox = flummox. That's it — a sick ox, one with the flu, right?

Of course, it's entirely plausible that unforeseen events will create inexplicable consequences.

Can't you tell I know EXACTLY what I'm saying?

If that were true, this would be a VERY different kind of notebook. Unfortunately I've discovered you're never too old to put your foot in your mouth.

Or to embarrass yourself in some other horrible way. Though with me it's things I say that seem to be the worst. Sometimes I want to rewind time so I can NOT say how much I played with troll dolls when I was little. Who wants to admit to that? What possessed me to blurt that out to a complete stranger next to me in line at the cafeteria. What was I thinking?!!

It's all the hairnet lady's fault. Her blue hair reminded me of my favorite troll, Bluebelly. →

She looked like a troll!

Try the meatloaf today. It'll stick to your ribs.

And she talked like a troll!!

So this notebook, which started out as a middle school journal of all my amazing middle school achievements, is instead a safe place to hide all the things I wish WISH WISH had never happened. If I put them down on paper, maybe I'll get them out of my head and I won't blush just thinking of them all the time.

Then I can focus on the good parts of me in middle school.

Amelia's Embarrassing

Moments Hall of Fame

Still, all in all, middle school is a BIG improvement over Little Kid School (or elementary school, I should say). And today our science teacher, Ms. Reilly, said something that made it even better.

I don't know about the bonding part. There are plenty of kids in this class I DON'T want to know any better than I already do. But the rest sounds good. So long as I don't have to share a room with someone who snores, burps, farts a lot, or talks in their sleep. And so long as I DON'T have to sit next to someone on the bus who gets carsick or sings loudly off-key. In other words, so long as I don't have to travel with anyone like my sister, Cleo.

KIDS TO BE AVOIDED — ESPECIALLY AS PARTNERS FOR ANY KIND OF PROJECT

↓

Sean — he always weasels his way out of doing his share.

Hee, hee... how about you do parts A and B and I'll do C and D?

Too bad there are no parts C and D.

Linda — she means well, but she's so anxious about everything, she drives you crazy!

We've got to be organized. I'll make a list.

No, two lists. Wait, should that be in alphabetical order?

How about index cards? Those are useful.

Paper clips! We need paper clips! Lots of them!

Charlotte — she whines so much, it's like her underwear is always too tight (or maybe it's her headband).

I would have written more, but the sun was in my eyes and my hand got a cramp...

...and then I lost my favorite pen. It was impossible!

Chris — he never can remember when assignments are due.

The report is due TODAY? I thought we had till next week.

Isn't today Tuesday?

You mean today is Thursday?!

I like Ms. Reilly. She's a good teacher. — for one 45-minute period. What will it be like spending 3 whole days with her? Maybe too much of a good thing.

She's the kind of enthusiastic teacher who is so excited by what she's talking about, she thinks you must be too—so before you know it, you're hearing details about stuff you never wanted to know.

The first few minutes, it's fascinating. Then it's bearable. Then for the last 10 minutes it's too much — your brain is overflowing.

This is a perfect example of Fibonacci numbers. You don't count the bracts but the spirals winding around the pinecone — clockwise, counterclockwise, it doesn't matter. You'll end up with Fibonacci numbers. Every time. Every pinecone. How does nature do it? Is Mother Nature a mathematician?

Now you ask, what ARE Fibonacci numbers? Let me explain...

← MORE Fibonacci numbers →

I'm NOT asking! I'm too busy counting spirals, losing track, and counting all over again.

We won't just be bonding with each other — we'll be bonding with our teacher. Good thing this field trip isn't led by Mr. Lambaste, my evil English teacher. Ms. Reilly may talk a lot, but she's NICE. Anyway, it would probably take three days with her for me to finally get what she's talking about when she says "Fibonacci."

I've never been with a teacher for that long, and I've never gone on a field trip where you sleep there. That's another new thing about middle school, I guess. I wonder what the beds will be like... and the food. Will I have to take showers with everyone else? Will kids make fun of my pajamas? What am I getting myself into? I made a quiz about that once, how what you wear to sleep reveals your personality whether you want it to or not.

THE PAJAMA GAME

Pick out the sleepwear you like best. Choose some slippers and a bathrobe to go with it. The combination you pick says a lot about who you are!

Ⓐ furry, zip-up pajamas

Ⓑ your clothes (why bother to change?)

Ⓒ oversized T-shirt

Ⓓ top and boxers

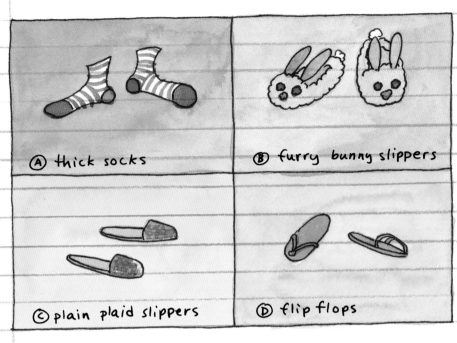

Ⓐ thick socks   Ⓑ furry bunny slippers

Ⓒ plain plaid slippers   Ⓓ flip flops

Ⓐ long terry-cloth robe   Ⓑ flannel robe

Ⓒ old hoodie   Ⓓ fancy kimono

If you chose mostly A's, you like to be warm and toasty.

If you chose mostly B's, you like things to be easy and convenient.

If you chose mostly C's, you don't get cold easily.

If you chose mostly D's, you wear whatever your mom buys you.

If you chose a mix of all the letters, you have a very distinctive style!

And if you're getting sleepy reading about pajamas, then it's time to go to bed.

Gggg nnakk!

← Cleo snoring in whatever she happens to be wearing

I wonder what kind of pajamas I should pack. Maybe I should get some new ones just for the trip. I'll ask Carly what she's bringing, and that's what I'll do.

Carly's really excited about this field trip. She says it's going to be great.

I hadn't even thought of that part! It'll be like a vacation from home! No rude noises from Cleo, no more smelling that nasty stuff she uses to strip the hair off her legs, and no more listening to her terrible singing (screeching, I should say). And it'll be a break from Mom, too. No nagging to clean my room, floss my teeth, or do my homework, and if I don't want to eat rubbery green beans, I won't have to. Teachers care about homework, not vegetables left on your plate.

I was really getting excited about the class trip...
up until tonight at dinner, when something happened
that changed EVERYTHING! Horrible, horrible
news — my life in middle school is doomed,
DOOMED!

Cleo said the WORST thing that could have
possibly come out of her mouth.

I almost choked on my macaroni! Cleo working with my class? That's my worst nightmare! She's EXACTLY what I want to avoid on this trip! It's a collision of worlds!

school world ↓

home world ↓

ocean of homework
art class
gym
friends
cafeteria

sea of chores
kitchen
family
island of my room
living room
bath-room

The only worse-case scenario I can imagine is if Mom became one of my teachers — that would be a supernova!

I can just see Mom saying the WORST things in front of everybody! ↓

Amelia, did you brush your teeth this morning?

You're not wearing the panties with the holes, are you?

And Mom seemed to think it was great — as if I want Cleo with me. Doesn't she understand what a DISASTER this is? Way worse than a 10.2 earthquake or hurricane force winds!

I'm not sure which would be more embarrassing - hearing Mom say "panties" or everyone knowing about my holey underwear.

Isn't that nice, Amelia? You'll have your sister with you.

She can watch out for you and make sure you're okay.

Mom gets more clueless the older she gets. When has Cleo EVER taken care of me? And why would I need her to anyway? I can take care of MYSELF! And if I couldn't, Cleo is the LAST person on earth I'd want to depend on!

Cleo was so happy with what Mom said, she practically purred. She KNOWS I don't want her around, and she's GLOATING!

Of course I can, Amelia, and all that sisterly togetherness will be wonderful. PURRRR!

I WANTED TO PUKE!!

Mom and Cleo both looked at me, waiting for me to say something. Only there was nothing to say, not to them. I just mumbled that I had a stomachache and asked to be excused from the table. Once I was safe in my room, I did the only thing I could think of —

I called Carly in a panic.

What am I going to do? I'll get the flu! I'll have to stay home! ANYTHING but going with Cleo! She'll ruin my life— I KNOW she will!

Calm down, Amelia. Don't you think you're overreacting? So what if Cleo goes too? She's an aide. She won't be in charge of you.

Yeah, but before I had to worry about a teacher hating me because he'd taught Cleo and assumed I was like her, a mean trickster. NOW I have to worry about the kids in my class meeting my gross, rude sister and assuming I have the same disgusting habits. It's a NIGHTMARE!

Maybe that won't happen. I've met Cleo, and I don't think you're at all like her just because you're sisters.

You don't know Cleo like I do. She's HORRIBLE! She'll do SOMETHING to embarrass me — she can't help it, it's part of her genetic code!

Carly didn't get it. How could she? Her brothers are normal—not creatures from the black lagoon, like Cleo. It's bad enough I have to live with her. Does everyone have to know we're related?

I wrote to Nadia. Even though she's an only child, she'll understand. She knows what a disaster Cleo is. ↘

Dear Nadia,
Here I am in middle school, where ~~suddenly~~ your reputation really ~~matters~~, and I have to deal with Cleo contagion. Normally we only ~~see~~ each other before and after ~~school~~, but NOW ~~she's~~ a student helper on our ~~class~~ science trip, ~~so~~ we'll be together __all__ the __time__! How can I survive unscathed? It will be the ~~most~~ embarrassing field trip of my life!

HAVE A SEAT

23¢

Nadia Kurz
61 ~~South~~ ~~St.~~
Barton, CA
91010

Yours till the mouse traps, Amelia
HELP! S.O.S.

It'll be like kindergarten all over again, only instead of having girl cooties, I'll have Cleo cooties.

Ay, ay, ay...

marshmallow pie, ay, ay...

Spit in my eye, eye, eye...

← bad, off-key singing—head for the hills, quick!

I tried to tell Ms. Reilly that I might have to miss the field trip, but my brain didn't work fast enough to think up a convincing excuse.

Lying to teachers is like lying to parents — you can't let them smell your fear! If _you_ believe your lie, then _they'll_ believe it, but if a _hint_ of doubt creeps into your voice, the game's up and you've lost.

Um, Ms. Reilly, I'm afraid I'll have to miss the class trip. I'm really sorry.

Miss the trip? Of course you won't! Unless you're in the hospital— and you look fine to me.

It's just that, um, my dad will be visiting from out of town and I don't want to miss him.

And I'm sure your dad wouldn't want you to miss the trip. How about I call him up for a little chat?

NO! I mean, no, that's okay, I'll ask him myself.

You do that then. And if he says you can't go, I'll ring him up and we can discuss it.

SIGH!

What a disaster! There's no escaping Cleo! I had the worst headache ever today.

Carly's still trying to convince me everything will be fine. Mom insists it will all be wonderful. And Cleo, even Cleo, suddenly seems to imagine we're a different kind of sisters than we really are, like she's been watching too many sappy movies about sisterly love.

Of course, Cleo's probably saying this to impress Mom. I know she's trying to convince Mom to let her take the bus into the city, and she's going out of her way to show how responsible she is — like emptying the dishwasher <u>before</u> Mom asks her, taking out the garbage when it's not even her turn, and now acting like a sweet big sister when she's NOT!

But no one asks me what I think, what I want — and what I DON'T want. Top of that list is "bonding" with Cleo. I don't want to be in the same room as her, much less get close to her! And she's never wanted to be friends with me, either. What's all this lovey-dovey, nicey-nice stuff about? It's got to be a trick, a way to get on Mom's good side, and NO WAY am I going to help Cleo with that! But I have to be careful what I say in front of Mom, or <u>I'll</u> look like the mean, bad sister, when really that's Cleo.

How can I beg to stay home now? HOW CAN I GET OUT OF THIS?

I'M DOOMED!

Tonight at dinner I felt like a prisoner having her last meal before being led to execution. Tomorrow we leave for the class trip. I still haven't heard from Nadia, and it looks like there's no escape.

Lying in awake in bed, I tried frantically to think of a way out.

I could turn off Mom's alarm clock so she would oversleep and we'd miss the bus — except Mom wakes up even without the alarm.

I could paint dots on Cleo's face while she sleeps so it looks like she has chicken pox — except she's already had them.

I could pretend to have acute appendicitis except Mom would never believe me — she's not trusting that way.

OW!

I was trapped. Only a miracle could save me, like a sudden mudslide blocking the road to the science camp or all the teachers going on strike.

I wanted desperately to stop time, but morning came anyway. Even though I deliberately left my backpack in the house so we'd have to come back and get it and miss the bus, Mom noticed I didn't have it with me and made me put in on and marched me to the car. There really was no escape.

At least Carly was happy to see me.

Amelia, over here! Let's make sure we sit together on the bus.

I admit I was glad to have someone waiting for me. Especially since Cleo didn't. I mean, it's my class, my friends. Except that meant without her own friends to join, Cleo stuck to me — like glue.

Cleo's glue-all - for instant bonding or sticky messes

On the bus I got to sit next to Carly — good. But then Cleo  got on and sat next to me — bad. Luckily Carly had brought her MP3 player and extra headphones so we could listen to music and not Cleo — good. Unluckily Cleo got carsick like she always does — bad, VERY bad! And the window on the bus wouldn't open — WORST OF ALL!

This is going to be a very long class trip.

And the teachers didn't make things better. Ms. Reilly and Mr. Wu, the other science teacher, took turns leading us in stupid games like science trivia. Like who invented penicillin and what is it anyway? Cleo naturally didn't answer a single question — she was too busy with her barf bag. And Carly and I were concentrating so hard on NOT breathing, we didn't get any right either. It's hard to think when you're trying NOT to smell, taste, see, or hear what's right next to you.

LET US OUTTA HERE! HELP!!

At last we got to the ranger station at Drake's Beach. Carly and I practically threw ourselves out of the bus. We gulped in fresh air like we'd been drowning (drowning in Cleo fumes, that is). I never knew how good salty ocean air could taste!

Cleo looked so pale and exhausted, I almost felt sorry for her. →

Almost. ↙

Cleo was so weak, she couldn't even carry in her duffel bag so I had to do it. Hah! Here she was supposed to be looking after me, and I ended up taking care of her! Shows what Mom knows! I was right — there's no good part to having Cleo here. It's bad, bad, all BAD. Bad beginning (a vomitrocious one!), bad middle, and bound to end badly (there's always the barfy bus ride back).

After we put our stuff away in the dorms, we were divided into groups and met our teachers. Even though Ms. Reilly and Mr. Wu came with us, they won't lead the classes. Instead they'll work with the instructors here.

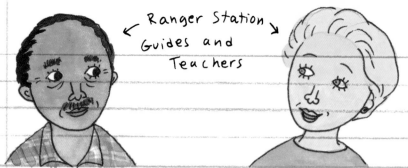

← Ranger Station →
Guides and
Teachers

Mr. Welkin has a warm, friendly face. He looks like someone who spends a lot of time outdoors.

Ms. Cook is young and enthusiastic. She just started teaching but seems like she knows a lot of stuff.

Ms. Reilly (and the other teacher from our school, Mr. Wu) will go from group to group. →

She'll spend half her time with Mr. Welkin and his students and half with Ms. Cook and those kids.

We have a lot to cover in three days, so you need to really listen! You'll learn about the tidal zone and the fascinating forms of life that thrive in this unique environment.

I just hope I thrive, not wither away, sharing my environment with Cleo. Maybe she had to come on the trip, maybe I have to sleep in the same dorm as her, but I could still pray she wouldn't be assigned to my group. She could help the other 6th graders and leave me alone.

But before the 8th grade aides were assigned, we had to find out which group we'd be in, Mr. Welkin's or Ms. Cook's.

GOOD NEWS!

    Carly and I were put in the same group! We're both with Mr. Welkin. I was so busy worrying about Cleo, I forgot to think about the possibility that Carly and I could be separated. We're lucky that didn't happen. Then we waited to hear which 8th grader would help our group. I kept chanting in my head:

I guess the fresh air made Cleo feel better because just when I felt awful, she looked completely recovered.

← In fact, she was sickeningly perky.

Hey, Sis, looks like we're in this together!

Now I can really watch over you like Mom wanted. Aren't we LUCKY?!

Yeah, I wanted to buy a lottery ticket, I was oozing so much good fortune.

Funny, when I first started going to the same school as Cleo, she pretended she didn't even know me. Now that she's conveniently far away from her friends, she's all buddy-buddy. She's NEVER called me "Sis" before.

So why start now? Maybe she's trying to impress the teachers, especially after being NO HELP at all on the bus (just a source of toxic pollution). Maybe she's trying to prove she CAN take care of me after I had to lug her duffel bag for her. Whatever it is, I don't buy it.

She can't suddenly call me "Sis" and have me believe we're all lovey-dovey. Times have changed. She hasn't loved me since I was a baby and she called me "Pumpkin."

Then I grew into a toddler and started grabbing all her toys, and she called me "Brat" and "Pig-O."

Then I started school and learned to read and had my own friends, and she called me "Dummy" and "Booger."

Now I'm "Sis"? I don't think so!

No matter what <u>she</u> calls <u>me</u>, no way am I calling <u>her</u> "Sis." I do have a lot of other names for her, though.

Mostly I call her "Jelly Roll Nose" — she hates it.

Sometimes I call her "Crumb Volcano" because of the way she spews when she eats — GROSS!!

When she's really mad, I call her "Snort Face" because of the delicate way she expresses anger.

I have only one choice for survival — I'm NOT going to be "Sis." I'll have to pretend Cleo is invisible. (That or I'll have to be invisible.)

That means enough writing about Cleo. It's time to think about this place, Marina Headlands. It's like a nature center, only with classrooms, dorms, and a cafeteria. Each day we'll do some science, some arts and crafts, and a nature hike. But the biggest challenge (besides the slimy showers and smelly toilets) is the climbing wall.

side view of climbing wall ↙

Using the bumps on the wall as handholds and footholds, everyone tries to climb as far as they can. You're supposed to make it all the way to the top, but so far no one has. Well, it's only the first day; I'm sure we'll get better. →

Usually I'm the worst in the class in sports because I'm so short and small, but I actually made it up the wall farther than anyone else. Finally, an advantage to having less body weighing me down! Carly did pretty good too. Cleo was predictably pathetic. She never does ANY sports. ↙

Unfortunately Cleo isn't cooperating with my invisible plan. She's all TOO obvious. There's no way to avoid her from the beginning of the day to the end.

Then we had to get ready for bed, and I remembered all the things I had worried about <u>before</u> I knew Cleo was coming — real worries like getting undressed before everybody and having the right pajamas and sleeping in a strange bed and hearing scary noises at night.

Good thing I had Carly with me. She let me borrow a pair of her pajamas, so I wouldn't look dorky. (Carly's automatically cool. I don't know how she does it, but she is.) I changed as quickly as I could without looking at anyone else changing (that old magical trick of thinking if you can't see someone, they can't see you). Then I got into bed and since I was safely covered, tried to see what everyone else was doing without looking like I was looking.

It was a fascinating study in itself.

Sharleen brought 6 pairs of pajamas for 3 nights and spent 20 minutes deciding which ones to wear.

Lucinda put some green goop on her face and went to sleep like that.

Jessica brushed her hair 100 times— She actually counted out loud to be sure.

Maggie was very embarrassed when she put on complicated headgear for her braces. It looked like a medieval torture device and she looked totally tormented.

Sue wasn't at all embarrassed about clipping her toenails— GROSS!

Charisse, who's so perfect about everything, wore slippers that matched her nightgown and had a cute little light to clip onto her book so she could read.

And Cleo? ➜

← I already knew about Cleo's bedtime habits and now everyone else would too.

First she popped her pimples, then she rubbed some evil-smelling goo on her face, then she changed into boxer shorts with hearts on them and a bright pink T-shirt that said "BIG MAMA" on it, then she bellowed "Sweet dreams, everybody," waking up a couple of kids who had already fallen asleep, then she did what she always does, every night for as long as I've known her.

She snored.

It's been a long time since Cleo and I shared a room.
I forgot how loud she could be. Carly and I hardly slept at all.

How long will this go on?

I hate to tell you — the whole night.

Charisse, of course, had earplugs.

I was tempted to grab them out of her ears and put them in my own.

At 7 a.m. sharp the Cleo alarm went off, and it was time to start the day again. I don't know how I'll survive this week.

Everyone was groggy and exhausted at breakfast from sleeping so badly. Except for Cleo. And Charisse. Before we had a chance to really wake up, Ms. Reilly came to our table, eager not to waste one precious educational minute.

I was hoping we could start with a nice, easy art project. Eight in the morning is too early to face science and all of Ms. Reilly's facts. By 9 a.m. we were at the tide pools, which would have been fine if we could have just wandered around and looked at different sea life, but we had an assignment. "Serious work to do" according to Ms. Reilly.

I used to think science was a lot of fun, but today I learned a science secret — it's 50% fun and 50% booooooooooooring. The good part was the hike along the tide pools. At least I thought it was fun. Sharleen complained about getting sand on her shoes. I could understand if it was getting in her shoes, but on her shoes?

Then came the boring part. And even more sand — on our hands this time. Sharleen looked REALLY grossed out. Maybe it wasn't because of sand. Maybe it was because we had to collect snails. Not regular snails, sea snails. Our group found a lot of humor in that, due to the shell's resemblance to a certain someone's nose.

Hey, Cleo, your nose is running —

— away from me!

Wow! noses are everywhere!

I'll sniff one out!

Cleo was NOT amused. →

Mama!

At first I thought the nose jokes were funny, but then they got to be too much, even for me.

Hey, Amelia, what's it like to live with Cleo? Do you have to shield yourself with an umbrella every time she sneezes?

I bet you can't hide any secrets from her. She's sure to sniff them out.

Is Cleo giving you special privileges since you're sisters — like letting your nose out the rest of us?

Hey, Cleo's helped _me_ find lots of snails — she really has a nose for it.

Not that I felt sorry for Cleo — I felt sorry for _me_. I wished I didn't have a sister. I wished she would be buried by a sand dune or swallowed by a wave.

But she wasn't. And instead of trying to be less obvious, the way I would be if people made fun of me, she started making her own jokes.

Listen, if you had a nose like mine, you might be sensitive too. After all, my nose can smell the jam between my toes without me bending over.

My nose is so big, the airlines charge me excess baggage for it. It's so big, I can stand in one time zone and blow my nose in the other.

My nose is so big that when I snore, not only do I feel the bed shake, everyone else in the room does too! My nose is so big that when I stand sideways, it looks like a nose wearing a face and not the other way around.

I guess she thought everyone was laughing with her then, not at her. I'm not so sure. I just wanted to sink into the sand and disappear. Who wants a sister who's a clown? Or I should say, who wants a sister who's a walking, talking, snorting, snoring nose?

The thing about the ocean is, it's hard to stay mad or worried or even embarrassed near it. The air smells so good and the sound of the surf is so calming that you can't help but relax and have fun. Even Cleo couldn't ruin things. And I have to give her credit — she can have good ideas sometimes. After we had all found enough snails, she asked Mr. Welkin if we could play in the sandy part of the beach for a little while. He said yes, so we took off our shoes, rolled up our pants, and played tag with the waves. Cleo even did cartwheels! That got rid of the bad taste of all the nose jokes. Everyone just had a lot of fun. I guess that was the bonding Ms. Reilly was talking about.

Except Sharleen, the girl with all the pajamas, wouldn't take her shoes off. Tyler said it was because she was afraid of water. Corey teased her for being a coward. Lucinda accused her of being too stuck-up to play with the rest of us. Suddenly all the focus was _off_ Cleo and on Sharleen. I felt bad for her. Maybe Sharleen just doesn't like the feel of wet sand on her toes. After all, she doesn't like it on her _shoes_. If she's fussy enough to need so many pajamas, that could be her problem.

trail of footprints with one set of shoe prints →

When everyone put their shoes back on and we started walking back to the classroom with our pails full of snails, kids kept on teasing Sharleen until Mr. Welkin told them to quit it.

Are you in love with your shoes soooo much you can't bear to take them off?

Hey, do you wear those shoes to bed? I never see you take them off!

Are they glued on or something?

Sharleen looked straight ahead. I could see she was trying hard to ignore it all, but that's hard to do. →

Why didn't she just take off her shoes? Then everyone would leave her alone. The worst crime a kid can commit in middle school is to stick out. Even I know that!

I guess I should be grateful she took the attention away from me and Cleo. Seems like some kids, especially Tyler and Corey, need someone to pick on at all times. As long as it's not me, I should relax, but I can't.

Carly and I looked at each other. We were both thinking the same thing.

"Hey, Sharleen," Carly said, "slow down. We can't keep up with you." Sharleen looked surprised but she waited for us to catch up.

"Sorry about the shoe business," I said.

She shrugged. "It's ok. I don't care."

"The same way I don't care that my sister is the teacher's aide?" I asked.

She smiled and looked me in the face. "Yeah. Exactly. That kind of not caring." I rolled my eyes. "You know," she said, "she's really not so bad. It just seems that way to you because you're her sister."

Maybe. I'm not sure. But for a while at least, it didn't matter. I didn't think about Cleo at all. It was a great hike back. We talked about all kinds of things, Carly, Sharleen, and I. I think I've made my first new friend in middle school.

Maybe Sharleen's shoes give her confidence or maybe she's just got cold feet. It doesn't matter to me.

So that was all good. What came next wasn't. We went back to the classroom, each with a bucket of at least 50 snails, and we had to measure the opening in ALL of them. ALL FIFTY!! The point was to chart variations in growth in the snail population, but the whole time I was measuring, all I could think was WHY? What difference does it make? Was this one of those useless bits of information grown-ups insist you learn for no obvious reason?

STUFF YOU HAVE TO LEARN BUT WILL <u>NEVER</u> <u>EVER</u> USE
↓

aa

↑
the names of the state capitals— all the state capitals does after high school ANYONE ask you this? Isn't this kind of information what an atlas is for?

↑
negative numbers— they seem so crabby and mean (all that negativity), so why bother with them? Seems better to stay far away from their bad moods.

↑
cursive handwriting— come on, this is the computer generation. Who writes by hand anymore (except me in my notebook and I PRINT!)?

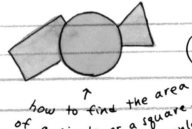

I'm really stellus magnificus.!

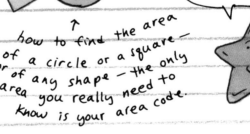

↑
how to find the area of a circle or a square— or of any shape — the only area you really need to know is your area code.

↑
measurements— does it matter if there are 2 cups in a pint? When do you measure a pint anyway? And who cares if there are 3 feet in a yard when most of the world uses the metric system?

↑
the scientific names for things — who calls a starfish anything but a starfish? Do you call a dog a canine? (wait, that's a tooth, isn't it?)

The first 10 snails were fine. The next 10 were bearable. By the 10 after that, I had to blink a lot to get my eyes to focus. I was seeing snails everywhere – not just double, but triple and quadruple.

← a blurry haze of snail shells →

There wasn't even a break at dinner. Ms. Reilly read us some of the other class's measurements while we tried to eat the dried-out meatloaf and gluey mashed potatoes. Talk about a way to ruin your appetite! Bad food + boring lists of numbers = a bad stomachache. At least the droning kept everyone's attention off Cleo and her bad table manners. Does she have to shovel so much food at once? Does she have to burp so loudly? Does she have to smack her lips? For once I wanted to hear every detail of Ms. Reilly's nonstop talking, even if it was about slimy snails. Anything was better than the sounds of Cleo eating!

Sharleen could see how annoyed I was. "Your sister's not so bad," she whispered in my ear. "You should see my brother – he's a master of chewing with his mouth open!"

Just then Cleo laughed so hard at something Lucinda said, milk shot out of her nose! That's WAY worse than openmouthed chomping. I wanted to crawl under the table.

why does it matter to me so much when she's the one who's gross?

After all, I didn't snort cow juice. I eat and drink politely. It's not fair that stuff I can't control reflects on me.

dripping milk from Cleo explosion

The ~~wiert~~ ~~weird~~ ~~wierd~~ weird thing is, Cleo didn't seem at all embarrassed. She just wiped her face and laughed at herself along with everyone else. Either she's being really smart or really stupid. I can't tell which.

AAAGH! I'll graduate college and still spell this word wrong!

"You still think your brother is worse?" I asked Sharleen.

She shrugged. "I can't help it — I admire Cleo's guts. Nothing seems to embarrass her."

"Exactly!" I said. "That's the problem!"

Maybe I'm just too sensitive. I admit that everything Cleo does seems louder and more embarrassing to me because she's my sister. I can't help it. Last night I dreamed of snails and Cleo all mixed together. It was a horrible combination.

HELP!

Measure me! I bet you can't measure up to me!

Cleo was a giant, and she kept yelling at me to measure her nose. I was afraid of falling into the black hole of her nostril, but I measured the opening just as she...

...sneezed!

I went flying in a cloud of snot, and right before I splatted on the ground, I woke up.

My teeth were chattering, I was so terrified. It took a long time before I could calm down enough to fall asleep again. The roar of Cleo's snores did NOT help. I didn't need to be reminded of the proximity of her nose.

I looked around the dorm room. It was so dark, everyone looked like mounds on their cots. I couldn't tell Sharleen from Carly, Lucinda from Charisse. The only person who was more than a lump of blankets was Cleo. She was a noise machine, the source of a growling

GNAKKAKKAGG.

It was like she was a giant nose, just like in my dream. I tried counting snores since I couldn't ignore them until my eyelids got heavy, and I must have fallen asleep because I had another dream. Cleo's nose was in it again, and it was even SCARIER!

In the dream I was in science camp, and Cleo was in charge of my group.

Only it wasn't really Cleo — it was her nose, a GIANT Cleo nose with legs and arms.

When the smoke from the sneeze cleared, Cleo had disappeared. Where did she go, I wondered. Then my nose started to twitch, to itch, to snort. I knew that snort! It could only come from Cleo's jelly roll nose! AND IT WAS ON MY FACE!!!

All the other kids started laughing and pointing at me. I pulled desperately at the nose, but it wouldn't come off. It just kept making farting noises. Even Carly was doubled over. Sharleen, too.

It was worse than the nightmares I used to have of going to school in my underwear! Everyone was laughing at me. And the nose **wouldn't** come off! When I woke up, I felt my face in a panic, sure my dream had come true. But there was my normal nose, right where it belonged. I was _so_ relieved, I felt I could face anything because at least I wasn't Cleo.   ← all the possible noses I could have →

Brushing my teeth that morning, lined up at the sinks with the other girls, it occurred to me that school is a lesson on how to handle embarrassing moments as much as how to solve math equations or understand history. Like public showers. So far _no one_ has used them here. Washing your face is one thing, undressing in front of everyone is something else. Maybe that's why Sharleen keeps her shoes on — this class trip is about more than bonding, it's about seeing parts of other students you really don't want to see. And I don't mean just parts of people's bodies. I mean private secrets that are hard to keep private when you sleep, eat, and spend all day together.

SECRETS OF
CLASS 6A

ABSOLUTELY
PRIVATE

NO UNAUTHORIZED PEEKING
ALLOWED

FOR AMELIA'S EYES
ONLY

Retinal scan being taken now!

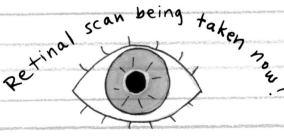

MY COLLECTION OF LITTLE-KNOWN FACTS PEOPLE WOULD PREFER TO KEEP <u>UN</u>KNOWN

↓

Carly sleeps with a retainer.

Kim has athlete's foot (<u>not</u> an athletic foot!).

Olivia hums when she brushes her teeth.

Lucinda wears underwear with days of the week written on them so she remembers to change them.

Maya actually likes the grandma-ish nightgown her mom makes her wear.

Carmen wears her brother's hand-me-down socks.

Vanessa keeps worry dolls under her pillow to keep away bad dreams (I need these!).

I WONDER WHAT KINDS OF SECRETS THE BOYS HAVE – I CAN ONLY IMAGINE.

Melvin never brushes his teeth (I bet this is true – I have a good hunch!).

Kirk only reads books when he's on the toilet (I don't know why he seems this type, but he does).

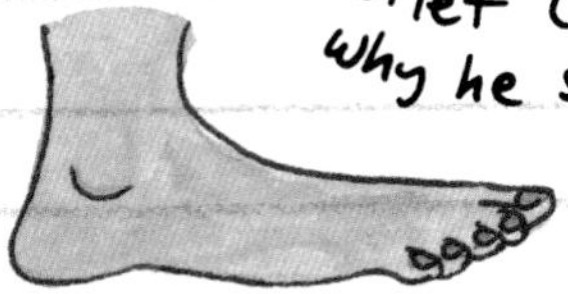

Jeff likes to paint his toenails blue – he borrows polish from his sister.

Sam practices his "looks" in front of a mirror – he's certainly polished enough.

Clark is Cleo's match in snoring – the way their names start the same is a clue.

← coyote

I guess we all have something to be embarrassed about — and my something is Cleo. At breakfast I sat as far away from her as possible. I thought kids would tease me about her. Instead they said nice things!

"We're lucky we got Cleo for our student aide," Corey said.

↑
black
bear

"Yeah," Lucinda agreed. "The other class got Kendall, and he's really bossy."

mountain
lion
↓

"I heard he made Carlos measure all 50 of his snail shells _twice_ because he was talking!"

"That's so unfair!" Maya said. "You can talk and measure at the same time."

"Cleo can talk and do _anything_ at the same time," Sharleen said. "And she's funny, too!"

↑
elk

skunk
↓

Could they really be talking about my sister?

After breakfast we went on a nature hike, looking for animal prints and scat (that's a nice, clean scientific word for poop). We found some raccoon prints by a stream but not much else.

↑
deer

deer
mouse →

← squirrel

↑
raccoon

It was turning into a dud of a hike. Then Sharleen wanted to rest —something about getting the sand out of her shoes (that girl and shoes!). Everyone groaned. Maya said Sharleen was holding the group back. Tyler said we should go on without her. But Cleo thought a break was a great idea. She plopped herself down on a boulder next to Sharleen.

"We've walked enough for a while," Cleo said. "Now we can wait for the animals to come to us instead of us looking for them."

I rolled my eyes at Carly. Yeah, right, we could just sit there and see nature if grass and trees were all you cared about.

Then suddenly Cleo stood up, pointing with one hand and waving with the other. I knew something was up when she did this SILENTLY. We all looked where she was pointing, and there stood the biggest deer I've ever seen.

Because it wasn't a deer — it was an elk! And behind it were more elk, a whole herd of → elk.

We all held our breath, it was so magical. I couldn't ← move. I just stared. Finally the herd melted into the forest. Gone.

It was the best part of the whole hike, and it was because of Sharleen and her sensitive feet. Maya walked next to her on the way back like she was her new best friend. Tyler said it was a good thing Sharleen was with us or we would have really missed out. I thought Cleo would want to take some credit for seeing the elk, but she didn't.

When we got back, I thought we'd have to chart the snail shell measurements we made yesterday, but Mr. Welkin didn't think we'd had enough activity.

Now that we've warmed up our muscles, it's time for a real challenge. By the end of the week I expect you all to make it to the top.

Let's see how many of you can do it now.

Most kids weren't exactly jumping with enthusiasm.

I used up my legs already.

Don't we get a snack first?

How about tomorrow?

I wanted to be the first to make it all the way, or at least the first girl. What I like about climbing is that a lot of it is mental, figuring out where to put your hand or foot next. The most important thing isn't whether you're strong or fast but whether heights make you nervous or not. Rule #1 is Never Look Down.

Naturally Cleo, the Carsick Queen, started sweating and shaking when she was only a yard off the ground. Sharleen tried to encourage her.

Everyone else started cheering her on too (except me). ↓

Go, Cleo!

Cleo power!

C'mon, Cleo, you can do it! Lead the way!

She almost got to the top. Almost. A couple of feet from it, Cleo stopped, just clinging to the handholds and footholds. The kids yelled even louder, but she was frozen. She shook her head and started back down.

The chanting stopped and a huge groan or sigh swept through the crowd. Then it was quiet. Too quiet. When Cleo stepped back on the ground, she looked like she was going to cry, but suddenly someone yelled one last "Cleo!" Kids cheered and the boy nearest her clapped her on the back. Another kid high-fived her. Cleo smiled and shook her head.

"Next time," she promised. "Next time for sure I'll make it to the top."

I have to admit I was impressed with Cleo. She started cheering for the next kid to try, Sharleen.

And there was no more grumbling about being too tired or wanting a snack. Now _everyone_ wanted to climb!

When it was my turn, I could hear Cleo yelling my name loudest of all. I was tempted to look at her, but I remembered rule #1 - NEVER LOOK DOWN! So I looked up and pictured everyone's voices as a big hand shoving me forward.

AND I MADE IT! I DID IT! ALL THE WAY TO THE TOP!!

Then I did look down. Cleo was smiling and waving and Carly was jumping up and down, all excited for me. For a minute I was so happy, I didn't even feel dizzy. It was funny - I felt like I'd climbed to the top for myself _and_ for Cleo.

YAY!! AMELIAAA!!!

Then I had to blink my eyes so the ground would stop moving. I focused on my hands in front of me, took a deep breath, and remembered what Mr. Welkin had said - I had to let go of the wall and rappel down.

Only my hands didn't want to let go of the wall and grab onto the rope. I was so high up, it was hard to trust the slender, swaying rope.

AMELIA AMELIA AMELIA

Carly had done it. Sharleen, Lucinda, Tyler, Max, and Omar had done it. Lots of kids had done it. I took another deep breath —

and I let go of the wall.

I kept my eyes on my feet, bouncing off the wall.

And bounce by bounce, I rappelled down to the ground.

IT WAS GREAT!!! I felt like I was flying! When my feet landed, it was like I'd taken a _much_ longer journey than 20 feet up a wall!

Carly ran up and hugged me. Cleo helped me out of the harness and said I was Supergirl. Sharleen said she knew I could do it. I knew that too. Today may have started with a nightmare, but it had turned into a fantastic, amazing, wonderful, incredible day!

That night when we were all in bed, Cleo broke the "no talking after 9 p.m. rule" (and she's the person in charge of _enforcing_ the rules).

"Well," she began, "I think that was my most embarrassing moment for the year — not making it even _close_ to the top of the climbing wall."

"More embarrassing than getting carsick on the bus ride?" asked Olivia.

"More embarrassing than blowing milk out your nose?" asked Lucinda.

"Definitely!" said Cleo. "I'm used to that other stuff."

There was a long moment where no one talked. Then Cleo asked, "So what's your most embarrassing moment? Here's your chance to get it out of your system. This is like truth _and_ dare — do you dare to tell the truth?"

The darkness was so thick, it made the quiet seem even louder.

More silence.

"Come on," Cleo urged. "It won't be so embarrassing once you describe it."

Part of me wanted Cleo to SHUT UP! What if she told an embarrassing story about _me_? Like the time I fell into the fountain or the time I followed a complete stranger around the grocery store thinking she was Mom (I was really little and grown-ups look similar from the knees down). Or the time I tried to hatch an egg from the refrigerator. I'd have no choice — I'd have to cover her face with my pillow. Even if she didn't spill the beans about the time I wore my shirt backwards for the whole day, I HATED that she knew all this stuff about me.

Besides all that, I couldn't stand her being all buddy-buddy with my friends. They can't like her AND me.

But part of me, the not-sister part, wanted Cleo to keep on talking. It would be fun in the dark to hear about the embarrassing stuff you could never talk about in the light of day. I didn't want to admit anything, and I sure didn't want Cleo to tell any incriminating stories, but I hoped someone would confess.

Then a voice said, "Okay, I'll start." It was Carly!
"Here's my most embarrassing moment. I was in 3rd
grade and playing tetherball during recess. I had on
a new skirt I really loved. I loved it so much, I wore
it even though it was a little big on me. I swung real
hard at the tetherball — AND MY SKIRT FELL
DOWN! I pulled it back up so fast, I don't think
anyone even noticed, but I sure did! And I kept
staring at everyone all day, trying to figure out if
they'd seen my
underwear or not."

← underwear!

legs! →

← completely
visible!

Everybody laughed. That broke the ice. Suddenly
everyone had a funny embarrassing story to tell.
I stopped worrying about Cleo and just listened and
laughed with everyone else. It was amazing that not
one of the stories made me cringe with shared
embarrassment. They were all just hilarious.

Embarrassing
Great and

The funny thing was, what really embarrassed one person didn't bother the rest of us at all. You think everyone's laughing at you, but no one thinks about it as much as you do. Like years later, Carly still blushed thinking about her skirt falling down, but no one else even remembered it.

And HOW did that bean get there?

getting a bean stuck up your nose and having to go to the doctor to remove it

what's that smell?

↑ tracking dog poop into your best friend's house

Oops.

Nighty night!

Sweet dreams!

thinking it's Pajama Day at school when it's really the NEXT day

Did someone see this? Please don't let anyone see this!

not watching where you're going and walking into a post — the physical pain is NOTHING next to the embarrassment

BURP

burping loudly during silent reading

Everyone had a story to tell.

"I stood up to give an oral report — and farted!"

"The teacher said my name wrong in front of the whole class. Instead of calling me Peggy, she called me Piggy!"

"I didn't mean to, but I sneezed in the teacher's face!"

"No one told me I had something between my front teeth, and it was school photo day. I tore up all my pictures but I couldn't change the class photo!"

I was laughing hard with everyone else until Maya noticed I hadn't said anything yet.

"Come on, Amelia," she said. "It's your turn."

I couldn't admit my MOST embarrassing moment because it's way longer than a moment — it's my whole life! It's having Cleo for my sister! But everyone in my class loves her now, so how can I say that? I couldn't. I didn't. But I had to say SOMETHING or I was about to suffer another embarrassing moment.

So I told about the time I went to a pool party, only instead of packing my good bathing suit, Mom gave me the ugly old lady one WITH A SKIRT!

I tried not to wear it, but somebody opened my bag and found it and then I had to put it on.

I didn't know they still made suits like that!

I didn't know they EVER made them for kids. I've only seen them on old ladies.

I've always hated that memory, but after I told the story, I laughed as much as the other kids. I guess we really are bonding on this trip, if that's what it means to know embarrassing secrets about people. Only they're not secrets anymore — or embarrassing. Now, they're just funny stories. At breakfast everyone was in a great mood, like they'd gotten rid of a heavy weight last night. Everyone except me.

Watching Cleo laugh and joke with the kids at the table, I had an amazing thought. ⟶

If Cleo wasn't my sister, would I like her? Would I think she was funny like everyone else did?

Why should she be embarrassed after all?
She was just having a good time.

Maybe the embarrassing stuff was part of me, not part of her. After all, I didn't have to wear Cleo like an ugly bathing suit. I didn't even have to sit next to her. I wasn't sure what to think anymore. It was easier to measure snails than figure this out.

Today we charted our snail shell measurements so we could see the variations in the snail population. Having it laid out in a graph like that was pretty cool. You could see how there was a big difference from one end of the scale to the other. Kind of like with people. I could make a _lot_ of interesting charts showing that range.

VARIATIONS IN HUMAN POPULATION

You could graph all kinds of things, from the physical —

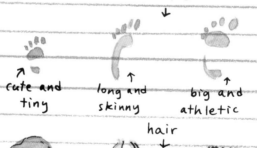

foot size
↓

↗ cute and tiny

↑ long and skinny

↑ big and athletic

↗ suspiciously large and clawed

hair
↓

↑ brown and furry

↑ blond and curly

↑ black and silky

↑ rainbow and fuzzy

noses
↓

↑ pert and small

↑ drippy and sniffly

↑ jelly roll and snorty

↑ pointy and in your business

That gave me the idea for a story.

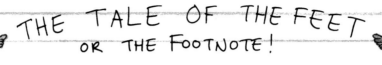

THE TALE OF THE FEET
OR THE FOOTNOTE!

Once upon a time there was a girl who NEVER took off her shoes. Even swimming she kept them on.

Look, Ma, I can still swim.

Even with heavy feet.

Everyone thought the girl was really strange, and because she wouldn't tell why she always wore her shoes, people made up their own reasons.

1) She had ugly calluses.

2) She had gross toe gunk problems.

what you get from cramming too-big feet into too-small shoes →

← more than toe jam — it's toe crust

3) She had the smelliest feet ever.

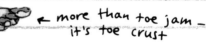

SAVE ME!

I don't want to go NEAR those feet!

The girl heard what people said about her.

And she didn't like it one bit.

The other kids didn't know what to say. After all, everyone was different in some way or other. But some differences were more embarrassing. Finally one kid spoke up.

The girl thought a minute. Then very slowly and deliberately she untied her shoes. She took them off. Then she took off her socks and stood before everyone with

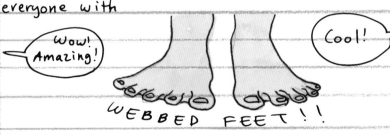

WEBBED FEET!!

Her feet weren't gross at all — they were really cool! The girl smiled. She loved the breeze tickling her toes, and the next day she wore sandals to school.

Not flip-flops, of course ←

She was like a whole new person — and she was definitely lighter on her toes!

Today was our last day and our last chance to try the climbing wall. I don't know why, but I heard myself saying, "C'mon, Cleo, you can do it! Go first and show everyone how it's done!"

Cleo shook her head. "I'm not ready yet. I don't want to be embarrassed two days in a row."

"What's a little embarrassment between friends?" I asked. I couldn't believe I said that — I was calling Cleo a friend! I'd NEVER done that before.

I guess she liked it, because she grinned and nodded. "Okay, here goes nothing!"

This time I was yelling with everyone else.

A wave of voices rose, pushing Cleo up, up, up. A couple of times she missed her footing, but she didn't fall and she didn't give up. She kept on going
ALL THE WAY TO THE TOP!

"You are so lucky to have her as your sister!" Sharleen said.

"See!" Carly nodded. "Cleo's not all bad. That girl has guts!"

"I know," I agreed. "I really do. Sometimes I just forget." I could see Cleo looking down and I worried she would get dizzy, maybe even throw up (that would be SO Cleo). But she kept on looking until she caught my eye. And she winked!

I couldn't help it. I yelled, "That's my sister! Way to go, Cleo!"

When Cleo got back down, a bunch of kids ran up to hug her.

I just stood and watched.

When the kids let go, Cleo walked up to me.

"Thanks, Amelia, for believing in me."

I nodded and felt my cheeks burn. Now I really was embarrassed but in a good kind of way. I felt something different, too, something I couldn't remember feeling before. I felt proud, proud of Cleo!

I stuck out my hand stiffly. "Good job, Cleo."

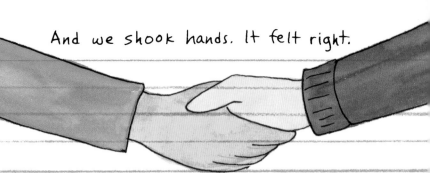
And we shook hands. It felt right.

I still didn't want to sit next to Cleo on the
bus ride home (her queasiness hasn't changed after
all), but somehow having her along wasn't as
annoying as before. The whole class sang songs and
took turns telling jokes and riddles. My riddle was:
what's the difference between a mountain and a
molehill? Answer: If you can't tell,
I'm not going climbing with you!

I made it to the top!

Big deal!

Ms. Reilly couldn't resist having a
captive audience (there's no escape on a bus!) so
she read to us from Darwin's voyage to the
Galapagos Islands on the Beagle. "Since we have
this time together, we may as well learn something —
right, class?"

Imagine all the snails on the Galapagos!

"Right!" we all yelled. One thing
we've learned is it's better to agree
with Ms. Reilly — or you'll get double
the information overload.

When I got home from the school trip, the first thing I saw was a postcard from Nadia waiting for me. ↓

Dear Amelia,
I know it's hard to get out from under Cleo's shadow, but you'll just have to make your _own_ shadow, if you know what I mean. People have to judge you for who _you_ are, not who Cleo is. If they don't, that's their ~~loss~~. Your friends don't think of you like that. Do the others really matter?
Anyway, I'm sure it won't be the most embarrassing field trip of your life. Remember the one to the jelly bean factory?

23¢

sitting pretty

Amelia
564 North Homerest
Oopa, Oregon
97881

luv, Nadia
yours till the
ink blots

As usual, she's right, even more right than she thinks. I've got to start seeing Cleo for who she is, just like I want people to see me. And I'm NOT going to be embarrassed by her anymore. She can embarrass herself all she wants, but from now on I'm in charge of my own embarrassing moments. I'm sure I'll have enough without taking on hers as well! And I don't have to let her cast a shadow over me. I'm standing in the sun, no matter what — with my shoes off and proud of it!

I forgot about pulling that lever and pouring 68 pounds of jelly beans all over the floor! That's a great story to tell! Next time... →

Amelia's Quick Guide to Surviving Middle School Embarrassing Moments

① Pretend that you don't notice that stain on your shirt. Or pretend it's a fashion statement.

② Act like you have toilet paper stuck to your shoe on purpose.

③ Laugh the loudest at yourself so nobody else can.

GENERAL MIDDLE SCHOOL SURVIVAL TIPS

① Never run the mile if your shoelaces aren't tied.

② Don't leave a tuna sandwich in your locker over the weekend.

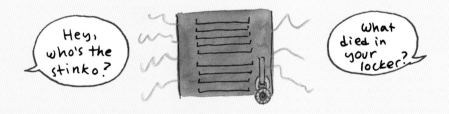

③ Don't EVER eat the cafeteria chili for lunch.

④ Write down your locker combination somewhere — you **will** forget it.

But now I have to remember where I wrote it. Someplace safe, I know - too safe!

⑤ Find someone to eat lunch with right from the first day.

Mind if I join you?

Great!

Sure!

Please!

Everyone's new the first week, so you have a good chance of meeting someone you want for a friend, not just eating company.

⑥ Be nice - you never know when you'll make a new friend, maybe for ALL of middle school - and beyond

You look familiar. Do you take the #11 bus?

Yeah, I do.

Want to sit together?

Amelia's

Guide to Gossip

The Good, the Bad, and the Ugly

by Marissa Moss
(and master storyteller Amelia)

Simon & Schuster Books for Young Readers

New York   London   Toronto   Sydney

Wow! The rumors are spreading FAR!

G is for Guess what's new!

G is for Gotta hear this!

G is for Gab!

G is for Gossip – and it's also for Guide, so this is a Double G notebook. I'm pretty good at guidebooks (this is my fourth – I've also made a Boredom Survival Guide, School Survival Guide, and Bully Survival Guide). But I'm not so good at gossip. I figure writing a guide like this will turn me into an instant expert. I want to know how to survive gossip (when it's about me) but also how to tell when it's true or not, how to enjoy it without getting into trouble, and how to turn an ordinary story into hot, juicy gossip.

Gossip can be like fire – mesmerizing to watch, but if you get too close, you can get burned. ➜

And if you're on the wrong side of it, you'll get smoke in your eyes. ↙

Like today — I heard this rumor and I wasn't sure if I believed it or not. Either way, I had to tell my best friend, Carly.

me
↓

Carly
↓

Did you hear about this? My English teacher, Mr. Lambaste, keeps handcuffs in the locked drawer of his desk and he uses them on students!

If you're bad — or if he just doesn't like you — he gives you detention in his room and handcuffs you to your desk for an hour!

Come on, Amelia! You believe that? He's mean, but not _that_ mean.

Yes, he is!

Then he would have done that to _you_ that time he gave you detention.

Maybe they're new — he just got them. Or maybe I was lucky and he forgot to use them.

"Besides," Carly argued, "that's illegal."
"Like he cares!" I scoffed.

"He doesn't want to get arrested or lose his job." Carly's always so calm about these sorts of things. I get all excited and she stays steady and practical. It's one of the things I love about her — but sometimes it can be exasperating.

So I kept on arguing back, in favor of the gossip. Really, it was too good _not_ to be true.

"Aha!" I said.

"Aha, what?" she asked.

"You didn't say it's something he _wouldn't_ do because he's not that horrible, just that he wouldn't want to get into trouble for it. That kind of rumor rings true because it fits — it fits Mr. L. perfectly!"

Even if some gossip isn't true, it can have an emotional truth to it. It can feel absolutely right! ↓

Carly's lucky because she has a normal English teacher. →

I'm stuck with Mr. L., who's always telling me what a bad student I am. He thinks I tried to poison him once with homemade cookies — that's how suspicious he is! ←

"Okay," Carly admitted. "You're right about that, but it still doesn't make the gossip true. This isn't news you're talking about — it's still gossip. Mean gossip."

Sometimes the line between news and gossip seems pretty thin to me.

"You shouldn't spread gossip unless it's true," she added.

"Then it would be all right?" I asked. "You said before that it's never nice."

Carly shrugged. "It's never nice, but it's a million times worse if you're telling lies."

In the case of Mr. L., I think it's doing other students a favor to let them know he's like this with everyone. Otherwise, they might worry they really were bad students. Really, he's just a bad teacher. →

I was relieved to find out that I wasn't the only kid he insulted. Not that I wanted someone else to suffer — I just needed to know it wasn't my fault — he likes to pick on kids. It's almost his hobby. ✓

And some gossip, even if it's true, you can't repeat or you'll get into trouble. Like a girl was sending nasty anonymous e-mails – REALLY mean stuff. Everyone knew about it, but no one wanted to be a rat and tell on her. We still talked about her to each other, but NOT to grown-ups.

Gossiping about her to other kids actually helped people. Like the rumors about Mr. L., it was a kind of warning. Of course, sometimes gossip is just fun, not at all educational, but if it doesn't hurt anybody, isn't that okay?

Carly says it <u>always</u> hurts the person being talked about because what makes gossip g<u>o</u>ssip is that it's about things people <u>don't</u> want known. Or it's personal comments that aren't nice. Saying "She's such a good artist!" isn't gossip, but saying "She draws on bathroom walls!" is. Sometimes it's hard to tell the difference.

Trust me – sometimes rumors NEED to be spread.

This is one of those times.

What's your source? Maybe you didn't hear right.

I trust you. I just don't trust the rumor.

I heard right — I'm sure of it. But Carly has a point. Sometimes a simple sentence can get really twisted when it passes from person to person, like in the game telephone, where you whisper something into someone's ear, they do the same, and with the last person you see how you end up with a completely different sentence than was started with.

That gives me an idea - here's a simple sentence test. Knowing that the rumor has been garbled and changed, pick which sentence you think is the original piece of gossip.

1. Sue's sadder legend quashed the fact.

ⓐ Sue had a hunch and washed her hat.

ⓑ Sue spat out her lunch and splashed the cat.

Mrrrow!

© Sue sat on her lunch and squashed it flat.

Oops!

2. Liam's locker smells like cold meat sandwiches half-filled with dog hair.

ⓐ Liam's locker smells like bony old witches have gone to dye hair.

Hee, hee, hee!

ⓑ Liam's locker smells like old feet and ditches half-full of diapers.

P.U.!

© Liam's locker smells like bologna sandwiches have gone to die there.

3. Maya sorted hairy budget sandpaper.

ⓐ Maya ordered magic card presents.

ⓑ Maya has suddenly smudged handprints.

ⓒ Maya has ordinary midget grandparents.

4. Hillary collects thread.

ⓐ Hillary stole Wesley's bed.

ⓑ Hillary sweats real bad.

ⓒ Hillary still wets the bed.

Answers:

If you picked mostly a's, you need to get your hearing checked.

If you picked mostly b's, you need to get your sense of logic checked.

If you picked mostly c's, you don't need to get anything checked — you have great gossip intuition and can tell the real thing from a muddled mess.

You mean "Maya has ordinary midget grandparents" is the real gossip? Are you sure? Sounds like mixed-up nonsense to me and I have a great nose for gossip.

But do you have a great _ear_ for gossip? Remember, gossip isn't necessarily _true_ information — it's gossip!

Which brings me back to what Carly said before —
how do you know if a rumor is true? And does it
have to be <u>literally</u> true or just true in a general,
vague way (like Mr. L. is mean to kids even if he
doesn't actually handcuff them)?

Carly says some gossip is like watching clouds —
it can change shape right before your eyes. One
minute you're looking at a dragon, the next a
giant floating ice-cream cone. I think it's more
like quicksand — the more you search for solid
ground to stand on, the farther you sink.

Up to my ears in slippery, shifting gossip.

Help!

There are different levels of shiftiness, different
degrees of probability. All you need is a scale to
measure each particular piece of gossip to give you
a sense of whether it's likely to be true or not.

Rumor Reading

Measure for Saturated Levels of Lies

10 — Totally provable – not a rumor at all, but a fact.
Example: Most kids don't like vegetables.

8 — Highly plausible, but not yet substantiated.
Example: The principal puts a black mark by the name of every kid who's had detention.

6 — Could be, but doesn't seem too likely.
Example: Locker 1313 is jinxed – if you put anything into it and shut the door, it disappears FOREVER!

4 — Nope, don't buy it.
Example: Cafeteria food is nutritious and delicious.

2 — Who are you trying to fool?
Example: The principal is cancelling P.E. for the rest of the year and replacing it with film criticism – watch as many movies as you like!

0 — Are you CRAZY?
Example: The most popular girl in school is Cleo.

Or you can use the Gossip Probability Factor Test.

1. Something is probably true if...

| (a) ...you hear the same thing from three different people. | (b) ...the whole school knows the rumor by the end of the day. | (c) ...you've never, ever heard anything like it before. |

You've already heard this?!

Can I tell you anyway?

Enough already!

WOW!!

2. Something is probably made up if...

| (a) ... a celebrity, a brand name, or an elf is involved. | (b) ... people laugh when they hear it. | (c) ...it reminds you of a movie you just saw. |

It's just not true!

You're kidding, right?

This is strangely familiar.

3. Something is based on some kernel of fact, even if it's exaggerated, if...

ⓐ... you know for sure part of it is true.	ⓑ...other people know for sure some part of it is true.	ⓒ... it just sounds true.

4. Something is definitely not true, even if part of it is based on facts, if...

ⓐ... it involves an alien.	ⓑ... it involves a buried treasure.	ⓒ...it involves a ghost, vampire, or werewolf.

Answers:

If the rumor fits mostly a's, it could very well be true. You can tell it to as many people as you want.

If the rumor fits mostly b's, it probably isn't true, but it still could be. If it's entertaining enough, go ahead and pass it on.

If the rumor fits mostly c's, there's a strong chance it's completely false. You can repeat it only if you warn people that it's not 100% fact (and it might not even be 1% fact). If it's interesting enough, no one will care about the made-up part.

Like the rumor the french fries in the school cafeteria are 30% cardboard, 20% eraser shavings, 10% salt, and 40% fat— the percentages might not be exact and there may actually be some potato involved, but the general idea is accurate enough.

yum! Dig in! ⟶

That tested the gossip. Now here's a test about _you_ –
your ability to tell good gossip from sour, rotting drivel.

1. You consider something is probably true if...

ⓐ ... everyone says it.	ⓑ ... it smells right to you.	ⓒ ... no one else believes it.

2. You consider something is not true if...

ⓐ ... no one else believes it.	ⓑ ... it smells fishy to you.	ⓒ ... everyone says it.

3. You consider a rumor to be based on some kernel of fact, even if it's exaggerated, if...

ⓐ... the cool kids say it.

ⓑ... it has no smell at all.

ⓒ... no one believes it.

4. You are totally confused and have no idea what to think if...

ⓐ... the almost-cool kids say it.

ⓑ... the smelly kids say it.

ⓒ...only the nerds say it.

5. You believe gossip that contains at least one of these elements:

ⓐ kissing	ⓑ aliens	ⓒ secret identities

6. You <u>don't</u> believe gossip that contains at least one of these elements:

ⓐ aliens	ⓑ secret identities	ⓒ kissing

7. You trust gossip depending on the...

ⓐ ... source.

ⓑ ... freshness.

ⓒ ... number of times it's been repeated.

8. You automatically don't trust gossip if...

ⓐ ... someone you hate tells it to you.

ⓑ ... the person who tells you hesitates a lot.

ⓒ ... the person who tells you is notorious for mixing up facts.

Answers:

If you chose mostly a's, you need to learn to think for yourself instead of always following the crowd. Either that or you love gossip so much, you want it all to be true.

If you chose mostly b's, you're an independent thinker with a keen sense of smell and a nose for news. Does that make you accurate in judging whether gossip is true or false? I have no idea!

If you chose mostly c's, you like to stand out from the crowd. Either that or you just don't trust gossip, no matter how probable it is.

If you chose a complete mix of a's, b's, and c's, you're as confused about gossip and how true it is as I am — sorry, I can't help you!

you can always use the coin flipping method when in doubt — heads, it's true, tails, it's false.

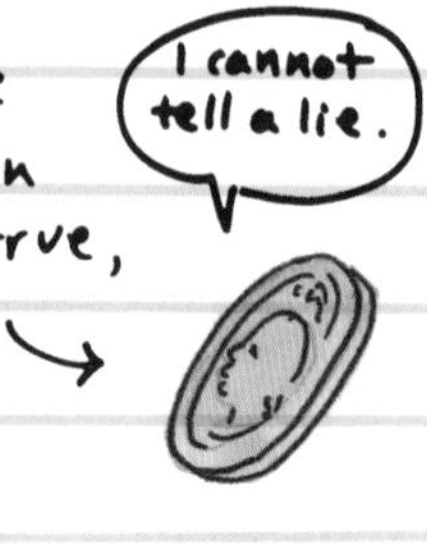
I cannot tell a lie.

The thing is, sometimes it doesn't matter if gossip is true or not — it's just a lot of fun. <u>That's</u> something Carly agrees with me on. We just don't always see eye to eye on what makes a great gossip item. Carly likes stories about famous people — the kind you see in magazines at the supermarket checkout stand.

Those are okay, but I like better the amazing stories about ordinary people — another kind of thing you see at the checkout stand.

Those are stories you can really sink your teeth into! It doesn't matter that they're obviously nowhere near true— in fact, that's part of what makes them so fun.

Carly wants to be a reporter when she grows up — like my dad. Usually she talks about being an investigative reporter, but sometimes she imagines what it would be like to write for one of those kinds of newspapers. Myself, I like inventing stories, not presenting information (that's boooooring), but I'd have fun being a reporter for gossip rags. We made our own once for school and called it "The Daily Dish."

The Daily Dish

All the news that's fit to make up.

Cafeteria Serves Radioactive Waste:

Glowing Spinach Tips off Science Teacher to Hazard

"I always had my suspicions," Ms. Reilly said. "The food there smelled strange, like chemicals rather than something edible." The cook refused to comment on the allegations.

Lost and Found: the Twilight Zone!

Objects go in, but they never come out! The growing, moldering pile of jackets, shoes, socks, notebooks, backpacks, lunch bags, umbrellas, books, pens, calculators, and all other objects turned into the Lost and Found are never seen again once they're put into the black hole of a closet. Once there, they all blend together.

GIANT EVIL DUST BUNNIES

Mildred Borstein never vacuumed under her bed, allowing the dust bunnies there to grow to monstrous proportions. Small stuffed animals that fell off the bed were devoured in seconds. The dust bunnies are now so large, they have taken over the 12-year-old's room, growling and snapping at anyone who tries to enter.

"I guess I'll have to sleep on the couch until I go to college," the girl shrugged, resigned to her homeless fate. Her mother, however, has not given up, and is planning a sneak attack tonight.

COCKROACH INFESTATION IN SCIENCE LAB

In an experiment gone horribly awry, eighteen large hissing cockroaches escaped from their cages and have now spread through the entire Math-Science wing. Impervious to poison or traps, the roaches now freely roam wild and have been seen in lockers, bathrooms, and drinking fountains. Students are advised to inspect food before eating it in case a cockroach is hiding there.

Normally, printed gossip has more weight and authority than the spoken kind — especially if there are photos. But I don't think anyone believed the stories we made up for The Daily Dish. That's okay — we didn't expect them to. It was just fun dreaming them up and then doctoring photos to go along with them. I wanted to do a special edition on urban legends, but Carly said those kinds of stories have been around so long, people actually believe them now (or kind of halfheartedly believe them), figuring there must be <u>some</u> truth to them if they've survived for so long. I still think they're gossip, just very old gossip that somehow never goes stale.

Most gossip has a very short shelf life. ↓

Not urban legends — they can live for years, even decades. ↓

Consume now while still juicy! →

Best when used by next week

Did Cleo really kiss Justin? Open the bag to find out!

Did a boy find a rat in his order of fried chicken? Open now for the answer!

Stay-fresh package keeps crisp for ages! ←

Urban Legends

Moldy oldies we all have heard ↓

↑ the lady who finds a
thumb in her bowl of
soup

Where can I
drop you off? Hey,
where'd you go?

↑ the hitchhiker who
turns out to be a ghost

If the phone hadn't
rung just then, I'd never
have escaped the fire! It
had to be my guardian
angel!

I knew she
really loved me—
I knew it! Now I
can die in peace.

↑ the letter lost in the mail
for decades that is finally
delivered at just the right
moment

↑ the mysterious phone call
that saves a life

There used to be a show on TV called "Fact or Fiction" that I loved to watch. It basically had a bunch of different stories — some urban legends, some true, some invented. At the end of the show you were supposed to guess which ones were invented and which were real. The thing is, the real stories seemed so fake, you'd never guess they actually happened. That's what made the show so cool — the real stuff was as unbelievable as the fiction.

Now with my handy-dandy gossip machine you can turn dry, boring day-to-day facts into the MOST EXCITING, UNUSUAL, DRAMATIC EVENTS POSSIBLE (as shown on TV in "fact or fiction")! Embroidery often does the trick — add new bits onto the old to make the dullest occurrence a sparkly adventure.

add bric-a-brac ↙

Old fact:
Maya fell and broke her ankle.

sew on fancy buttons ↓

New, improved version:
Maya was chasing after a bank robber and had almost caught him when he threw a heavy bag of coins at her. She tripped over the bag, fell flat on her face, and broke her ankle. The robber got away, but it turned out the bag was full of rare coins, way more valuable than the rest of the money the thief kept.

glue on glitter and sequins ↘

tie on ribbons and bows ↓

The bank was so happy to get the coins back, they gave Maya a reward for returning them, even if it was by accident.

I'm a hero!

Old fact:

Max spent the weekend visiting his dad now that his parents are separated.

New, improved fact:

Max's dad is in the FBI witness protection program and had to leave his family and move away. He's completely changed his identity with a new name, dyed hair, and a phony accent. Max waits at a designated corner until a strange car drives by and whisks him away to the secret location where his dad is now.

blacked-out windows so no one can see in

untraceable license plate

See, that stuff makes good gossip. The lowest level of rumors is the kind that's local – just in your school or family. But that can be the most interesting kind too, because you know the people involved. (Celebrities are people you think you know, but really you don't – you just know about them.)

The fresh gossip at school now is about the girl with the mean e-mails. Somehow the principal found out and we had to sit through a long, booooring assembly about NOT misusing e-mail. Everyone's talking about WHO told on the girl. No one knows, so a lot of different names are being suggested. That's not real gossip – it's speculation.

School has the MOST gossip, but there's a lot in families too. No matter who is in the family, chances are there's gossip about:

① The Black Sheep – Baaa!
   The person who didn't live up to expectations. They don't even have to be a criminal, just not the doctor everyone wanted.

② The Skeleton in the Closet –
   The secret everyone tries to hide.
   Boo!

It can be something really small, like Grandpa was married before and divorced wife #1, who is NEVER mentioned. Or it can be something really big, like Grandpa was married before Grandma to three different women and he didn't divorce any of them. Uh-oh! Grandpa's a bigamist.

③ The Buried Treasure —

Something of value that everyone in the family wants. Again, it could be something small, like Grandma's teapot. Or it could be something huge, like the family farm and 362 acres.

The best gossip needs to be both juicy and satisfying. Juicy gossip has some illicit tinge to it — the thrill of supersecretive stuff. Satisfying gossip isn't necessarily great gossip by itself but because of <u>who</u> it's about. There's something about the gossip that contradicts how the person acts or seems — which is EXACTLY what makes it so satisfying.

Satisfying Gossip

Mom is a total book snob — she says she only reads great classics or informative nonfiction, NEVER junk. But I happen to know that her lowest dresser drawer is <u>full</u> of cheap romance novels — the kind whose authors have names like Violet LaVoile or Star Meadows. This is JUICY and SATISFYING family gossip I'd love to tell <u>someone</u>, but if I did, Mom would kill me. (And that's NOT satisfying.)

> I can't put this book down — it's so exciting!

> There's nothing like reading the history of escalators.

Carly is a health food nut. She makes her mom buy organic groceries and she NEVER eats fast food. But I know she has a weakness for chocolate-glazed doughnuts. She allows herself one a week, which you would think wouldn't be a big deal, but she would die if anyone else found out.

Really, I only eat doughnuts to save some other poor soul from their fatty, greasy, sugary overload. It's a rescue mission.

Leah always teases people who play video games. She says they have batteries instead of brains and are like rats running through electronic mazes for a piece of virtual cheese. But she's secretly addicted herself.

This isn't _my_ Game Boy — it's my cousin's. And I'm not playing it — I'm just testing it for him. DON'T TOUCH!! You'll mess up my score. I mean, _his_ score. JUST GO AWAY!

Max pretends he doesn't like any girls, but I know he has a crush on Charisse. He sent her a secret valentine, but it ended up in the wrong locker — MINE!

My heart is beating so loudly, I'm sure she hears it. What'll I do? Should I talk to her? What if there's something stuck in my teeth?

That Max is cute — too bad he's not boyfriend material.

Charisse seems absolutely perfect in every possible way. She's pretty and stylish, dresses well, and has a British accent. What else does she need? But she has one fatal flaw — she chews her fingernails. With me that would be no big deal. With most people it wouldn't matter. To her it's a major blot on her image, a glaring defect she always tries to hide. Sometimes Charisse even glues on those fake fingernails. That's how I discovered her secret — one of her nails came out in her sandwich! It freaked me out!

← sandwich with fingernail garnish

Here's your very own handy-dandy guide to how hot is hot. RATE THE GOSSIP! Is it really hot, smoking, or mouth-wateringly JUICY?

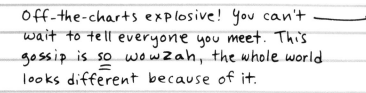

Off-the-charts explosive! You can't wait to tell everyone you meet. This gossip is so wowzah, the whole world looks different because of it.

Veeeeery interesting — your ears smoke just listening to it and your teeth tingle waiting to repeat it.

Okay, you're definitely paying attention. It's a warm little morsel — spicy, but not too hot.

It's a nice little appetizer and if the subject comes up, you'll probably repeat it. Otherwise you wouldn't bother.

A puff piece, not weighty enough to fill you up. Completely forgettable.

Why bother to say this? Who cares?

Dull, boring, a total yawn. This isn't gossip — it's a shopping list.

The absolute BEST kind of gossip is crazy stories about people you know <u>well</u>, like kids and teachers at school or people in your family. Cleo falls into both those categories, since she's still at my school and she'll always be my older sister (unfortunately).

When I got back from the big family reunion with my dad's family last month, Carly's first question was about Cleo.

It's funny that gossiping is called "dishing" — like you're serving up a delicious tidbit.

Cleo is the perfect subject for gossip because no matter what you say about her — the crazier the better — it still sounds like it could be true. Here's a Cleo fact-or-fiction test — see how well you can tell which stuff is made up and which really happened.

① Cleo likes to stick french fries up her nose.

Fact ☐

Fiction ☐

② Cleo once threw up on her science teacher, and he thought she did it on purpose.

Fact ☐

Fiction ☐

Is this some sort of bizarre experiment? I won't give you extra credit!

③ Cleo once went to school wearing her nightgown as an English project, saying she was Lady MacBeth.

Fact ☐

Fiction ☐

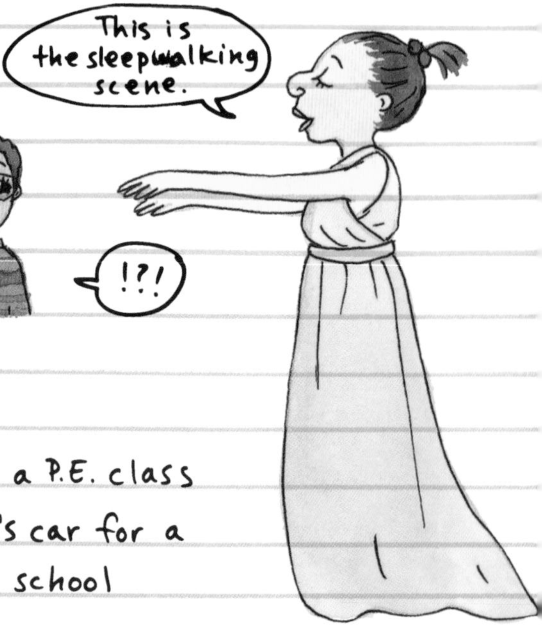

④ Cleo almost ran over a P.E. class when she took Mom's car for a practice drive in the school parking lot.

Fact ☐

Fiction ☐

⑤ Cleo dressed up as Madonna for the school talent show and sang "I Did It My Way."

Fact ☐

Fiction ☐

Waaaaaaay!

x-rated: cannot be shown on school property (really it's for your own protection— you wouldn't want to see it anyway, believe me)

⑥ For Cinco de Mayo, Cleo brought salsa to Spanish class that was so spicy, six students ended up in the nurse's office.

Fact ☐

Fiction ☐

Wow! Did the salsa burn a hole in the bowl?

You need a strong stomach for Salsa de Cleo!

If you said 5 questions or more were fiction, you don't know Cleo at all.

If you said 3-4 questions were fiction, you've probably seen my sister in action and have an idea what she's capable of.

If you said only 2 questions were fiction, you know Cleo well! You've got a good nose for the gossipy truth — dish it out while it's hot!

If you said only one question was fiction, why that one? If Cleo did most of those outrageous things, why not all of them? Or did you think the test needed one different answer?

If you said NONE of these questions was fiction, you're a GOSSIP WHIZ and Cleo expert and deserve the Golden Goose Award for Gossip Smarts!

why a goose? Are they gossip experts or just make a lot of noise? →

Of course, there's <u>another</u> kind of Cleo gossip — that's not gossip <u>about</u> Cleo but <u>by</u> her. Which is waaaaaay worse because usually it's about ME. That's one reason NEVER to go to the same school as your sister. Luckily my friends all know NOT to believe anything Cleo says. Unluckily that still leaves a lot of kids — and teachers — for her to infect. She's even gossiped about me with kids in Dad's family — cousins I hadn't met, so their first impression of me was through Cleo. Yucch! When that happened, I felt like I needed an extra-strength Cleo disinfectant to wash off the Cleo-colored reputation.

I wanted to scrub away the Cleo stain.

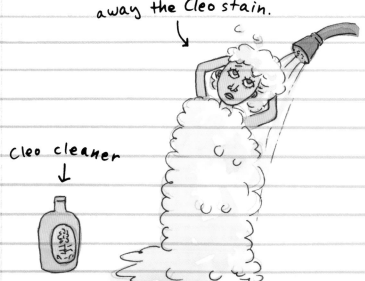

Cleo cleaner

That's the bad part of gossip — when people spread stories about you that are horrible lies and the more you deny them, the more people think they're true. But if you ignore the rumors, people will <u>still</u> think they're true. So how do you get rid of gossip when it's like stepping on a wad of chewing gum that sticks to the bottom of your shoe no matter how hard you try to scrape it off?

There <u>are</u> ways, but you can't do it alone. You need friends to help you — the more, the better.

How to Stop Gossip
OR RUMOR REMOVAL

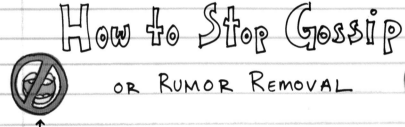

no yakking   ① Spread your own rumors   no blabbing

that are exactly the OPPOSITE of whatever the gossip says. The two things will cancel each other out.

② Have as many people as possible spread as many crazy stories as possible so NOTHING will seem believable anymore.

If the stories all intertwine, it's even better — MUCH more confusing.

Lucy is going to be on Teen Idol! She's lucky!

The new kid in French class is really a princess in disguise, like in that movie!

That new French kid is jealous of Lucy being on Teen Idol and tried to poison her so she'd miss the show.

Trevor ate 13 frogs in the science lab. He's gross!

Oh yeah? Well, the P.E. teacher used to work for the CIA interrogating criminals. He's a real torturer.

Did you hear about the P.E. teacher? He still works for the CIA. He's undercover, searching for a kid who hacked into government computers.

I heard that Trevor was trying to save Lucy from being poisoned, so he ate the frogs meant for her.

The new French kid cooked the frogs for Trevor to eat because in France, frogs are a delicacy.

No, you're wrong — Lucy ate the frogs as a stunt to get on TV. She's not on Teen Idol, but Survivor!

That's not what I heard! The frogs weren't cooked — the P.E. teacher scared Trevor so much, he swallowed the frogs thinking they had microchips inside of them. It was all part of the hacking case.

③ If those don't work, wait out the war or go into hiding, wearing camouflage.

Achoo! It's dusty down here!

④ Accept the rumor as true, but turn it into something good.

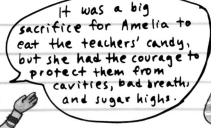

It was a big sacrifice for Amelia to eat the teachers' candy, but she had the courage to protect them from cavities, bad breath, and sugar highs.

How noble of her! Next time she should share the burden with me!

⑤ Accept the rumor as true, but turn it into something completely unbelievable.

That wasn't Amelia — she was abducted by a UFO and replaced by a fake Amelia who's really an alien trying to infiltrate our society — and eat its chocolate.

Oh, I thought it was Cleo pretending to be Amelia. She's pretty alien, though.

I can't believe this! Just when I'm writing about Rumor Removal, people are REALLY gossiping about me!

And they're not talking about candy. Kids are saying that I'm the one who got the e-mail girl into trouble. But I didn't! Why would I? She didn't send me a mean e-mail. I just heard about it like everyone else. I'm going for option #3 — hiding. If I stay in the library working on this guide, I can wait out the rumor — maybe.

Gossip about kids is one thing. Gossip about teachers is another. I know a lot of stuff gets made up about kids, but somehow the stuff about teachers always seems true, no matter how crazy the rumor. That's because really we kids know NOTHING about teachers except what they tell us and how they act in class. But there's always one student in every school who's got the dirt on all the teachers. If you want to know which teacher eats onion sandwiches for lunch (well, the breath is a BIG hint on this one), which one has a stash of comics in their desk drawer, or which one spends their summers playing in a rock band, you have to   ask the teacher expert.

In my school, that's Gigi. She's Cleo's best friend, but I don't hold → that against her — she's still cool.

Don't ask how I know — I just do!

← No matter how much you bug her, she won't give away her sources.

MATCH THE TEACHER TO THE GOSSIP

Mr. Lambaste

Ms. Oates

Mr. Le Poivre

Ms. Reilly

Mr. Klein

Mrs. Church

Has a second job being a clown at little kid parties.

Is married to another teacher in the school — who?

Lives alone with 38 cats.

Used to be a hippie, wear tie-dye all the time, and live in a commune.

Claims to have been abducted by a UFO in 1975.

Is going to law school at nights.

ANSWERS
(According to expert Gigi)

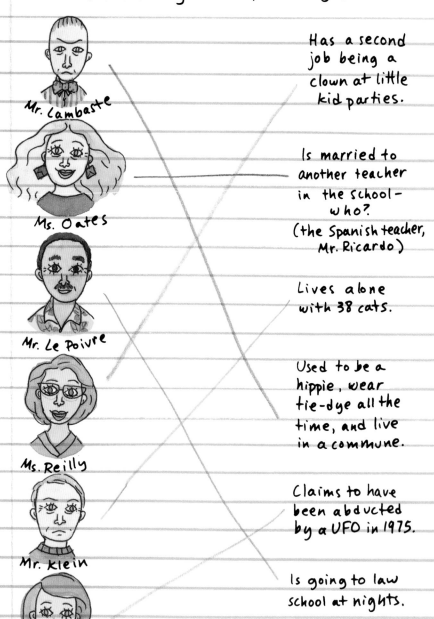

Mr. Lambaste — Has a second job being a clown at little kid parties.

Ms. Oates — Is married to another teacher in the school — who? (the Spanish teacher, Mr. Ricardo)

Mr. Le Poivre — Lives alone with 38 cats.

Ms. Reilly — Used to be a hippie, wear tie-dye all the time, and live in a commune.

Mr. Klein — Claims to have been abducted by a UFO in 1975.

Mrs. Church — Is going to law school at nights.

Strange but True!

What's the difference between gossip and trivia? If you tell trivia that you know about someone, does the act of telling turn it into gossip? Is gossip more a verb than a noun, or both equally? These are profound philosophical questions. Actually, gossip is all three things — the person who spreads it, the thing being spread, and the act of spreading it. The gossip gossips about gossip — get it? Is there any other word that is so multi-dimensional? Is there another word that can be the subject, the object, and the verb, all in the same sentence?

When I asked Carly about this, she said I was thinking too much.

I can't help thinking about gossip — especially now that it's about me. I'm afraid that once a bad story starts, it can only get worse. I mean, now people say I told on a girl for writing mean e-mails — what will they say next?

Yeah, I can think of another word like that — poop! The poop poops out the poop. See!

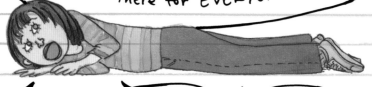

Can people really say that stuff? Can they believe it? What if no one will talk to me anymore? How can I rub out the rumors?

The problem is gossip travels in waves that are faster than the speed of light or sound. I can't outrun it or escape it — it's way too speedy.

Here's the proof: An ordinary conversation doesn't go farther than the people speaking to each other — that's the speed of sound. But one juicy whisper can be all over the school by the end of the day — that's the speed of gossip. It's completely unpredictable — saturating one area, leaving another untouched until suddenly EVERYONE's heard it.

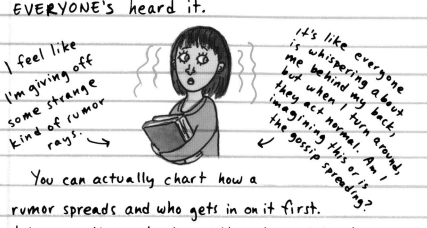

I feel like I'm giving off some strange kind of rumor rays. →

← It's like everyone is whispering about me behind my back, but when I turn around, they act normal. Am I imagining this or is the gossip spreading?

You can actually chart how a rumor spreads and who gets in on it first. Like everything else in middle school, it has to do with popularity. The cool kids get everything first, including gossip. The nerds are last, like they are in everything else. If the rumor about me ripples through the school like most gossip, soon the nerds and jerks no one talks to will be the only people I can be with — HELP!

The Gossip Ripple

The rumor starts here.

Immediately all the cool, in-the-know kids pick up on it.

The circle of kids who know the cool kids get in on it next.

Even the nerds have heard it out here.

Effect

The kids who aren't popular, but aren't unpopular either, are the biggest group of all. Once they hear it, it's all over the place.

The jerks no one likes or talks to know the rumor by now — they're the last to hear it.

This is a bigger group, so the rumor spreads faster.

Now there's no hope — the rumor is EVERYWHERE! who ever thought they'd be rippling about ME?

The jocks hear it in this group.

I guess that shows something useful about gossip — not that lies are spread about people (that's DEFINITELY not useful, especially when I'm the person being talked about) — but because gossip holds groups of people together and let's you see who's cool and who isn't. If you're not sure whether someone's a nerd or not (though usually that's VERY obvious), you can find out by seeing how much gossip they know. Or by hearing the kind of gossip that's said about them. So maybe it's good to be talked about. I need to remember that. It all depends on what is being said.

Bad Gossip
(the kind you DON'T want said about you.)

Personal Appearance   Personal Hygiene

Where DID Hilary get those shoes? They're from Dorkville!

She always wears the worst things! Have you seen her socks?

That Chris NEVER brushes his teeth — they're green!

EW! GROSS!

Good Gossip
(Even if it seems bad, it's good.)

Personal Relationships

He has such a crush on her!

Too bad she can't stand him.

Trendsetting

She started those pocket pets — now everyone has one.

That's better than those dumb rubber-band bracelets.

Hey! I have one of those!

Sorry!

Good/Bad Gossip
(It can go either way, depending on HOW it's said and WHO says it.)

Personal Idiosyncracies

She ALWAYS wears her shoes — even swimming.

What is that about?

Personal Habits

Is she naturally that skinny or is she anorexic?

I heard she's bulimic- it's scary!

Some psychologists actually did a scientific study about gossip (I swear, this is the truth — not a wild rumor!), and they discovered that not only is gossip a useful social tool for figuring out how to fit in with a group, you can learn some valuable lessons from rumors. Even if the actual piece of gossip isn't true, you can learn something from it. So when I'm gossiping, I'm actually expanding my mind. I like that idea!

Of course, when people gossip about <u>me</u>, I want them to learn good stuff, not bad, mean stuff. Maybe the thing they can learn from the rumor about me and the e-mail girl is NOT to trust gossip. That's useful too!

I told you gossiping wasn't nice. Now have you learned your lesson?

I wouldn't mind good gossip about what a good artist I am.

And sometimes you learn important stuff from gossip.

Well, some gossip isn't nice, but not all.

Important School Gossip You Need to Know

① Never buy lunch on Fridays — that's leftover hash day, when they take the food left over during the week, mash it together, and call it Chef's Surprise.

② The janitor closet in the 300 wing is haunted. Avoid it at all costs!

What are those strange noises?

c r e e e a k !

I don't know and I don't want to find out.

e e e e e e e k !

A kid opened the door to look once and was never heard from again!

③ The group of bushes in the far back of the soccer field are for the tough, bad kids. If you want to keep your money, don't go near them!

How much did you get from that kid?

One dollar and a subway pass.

What a waste! We need to go to a richer school!!

④ The 3rd toilet stall in the girls' bathroom in the 800 wing is a DISASTER — no one dares to use it.

⑤ Mr. Lambaste is the meanest teacher in the whole school. If you can get out of taking classes with him, DO IT! ANY teacher would be better than him.

See — not only can you learn from gossip, it can save your skin. It's way more useful information than the chart in the back of this notebook, which tells you how many pecks to a bushel or how many scruples to a dram. (I don't even know <u>what</u> those things are!)

Here's the test the researchers gave for YOU to take (along with my answers as examples).

① What is the most interesting gossip you've heard lately?

Hmmm, hard to say. Definitely NOT the one about me (boooring!) and the one about Mr. L. is so predictable, I'm not sure it's interesting. I guess I'd have to say Cleo kissing Justin in the barn at the family reunion.

Kissing is high on any gossip list anyway.

Cleo, puckering up

② Who was the gossip about?

a. a friend or acquaintance (most people said this)

b. a stranger (this was the next most popular answer)

c. a celebrity (celebrity was below stranger, believe it or not)

d. family (the fewest people said this — I'm unusual)

③ Did you pass it on?

a. yes (most people did, of course — me, too!)

b. yes, to more than 3 people (Fewer told this many people, but so far I've told 4 people about Cleo — Carly, Nadia, Leah, and Maya. What's the point of juicy gossip if you don't tell as many people as possible?)

④ Did the gossip reflect badly on the person being talked about?

Most people said yes to this, but in Cleo's case I'm not sure. Kissing is usually good gossip, not bad. And Justin is cute, so that makes it doubly good (for Cleo). But he's kissing Cleo and she's not cute, so that makes it bad (for Justin).

⑤ Did you learn anything that you can apply to your life?

Actually, I learned a few things.

1. Cute boys sometimes kiss not-cute girls. (This gives me hope!)

2. Cleo has some kind of charm that makes boys like her, though I have no idea WHAT.

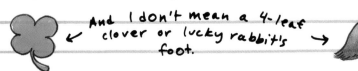

And I don't mean a 4-leaf
← clover or lucky rabbit's →
foot.

3. Kids may like gossip about kids kissing, but grown-ups DO NOT! (I don't know if they like rumors about grown-ups kissing, but they sure don't like the ones about kids kissing.)

This isn't the kind of test that has right or wrong answers. It's the kind researchers use to learn about a subject, so don't worry about saying the wrong thing. Anyway, with gossip there is no right or wrong, just more or less believable.

I learned a _lot_ of lessons from gossip — not just about Cleo, but about Mr.L., and, most of all, about ME. I learned I'm the kind of person who HATES to be gossiped about. It's not fun or exciting, like I thought it might be. It's ICKY!

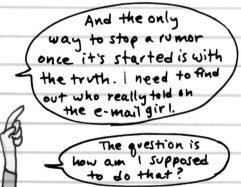

And the only way to stop a rumor once it's started is with the truth. I need to find out who really told on the e-mail girl.

The question is how am I supposed to do that?

Okay, I need a break from rumors, so it's time for a different kind of test. Again, there are no right answers, but there are <u>revealing</u> ones. Take this test to see

WHAT KIND OF GOSSIP ARE YOU?

1. Your favorite kind of gossip involves:		
ⓐ personal relationships.	ⓑ personal idiosyncracies.	ⓒ stuff that happens.

I heard he asked 3 different girls to the same dance!
I heard they asked him!
When she's done chewing her gum, she tucks it behind her ear.
GROSS!
That stupid toilet in the girls' bathroom overflowed again!
Double GROSS!

2. You like to gossip about:		
ⓐ cool people.	ⓑ nerds.	ⓒ jocks.

She was her friend until the new French girl came along - then she dropped her like a hot potato!
Too bad the French girl dropped her!
Can you believe he brought his magic cards to school? And he's asking kids to play with him?
He just likes showing off his collection.
The coach kicked him off the team last week for using bad language.
★#G✱!!

3. When you have a particularly juicy piece of gossip, you...

ⓐ...tell it only to your friends.

ⓑ...rush off to repeat it to the first person you see.

ⓒ...blurt it out at the wrong moment.

This is SO secret, only you can know.

Hey, you, STOP! I've got to tell you this! Listen!

Were you talking about ME?!

Oops!

4. You know a lot of gossip about...

ⓐ...who likes who.

ⓑ...odd details about people.

ⓒ...history.

You're wrong — she used to like him. Not anymore. Now she likes Trevor.

How do you keep it all straight?

Yes, she has a collection of rubber bands — really!

You mean those rubber-band bracelets?

No, just rubber bands!

Did you know people didn't wear underwear in the Middle Ages?

Now, that's hot gossip.

5. Your reputation as a gossip is...

| ⓐ... locked lips. | ⓑ ... not the most exciting. | ⓒ ... big blabber. |

6. The longest you've been able to sit on a particularly juicy bit of news is...

| ⓐ... one day. | ⓑ... one hour. | ⓒ ...one second. |

7. Your attitude toward the expiration date on gossip is...

ⓐ ... there's no point in not telling things right away – gossip goes stale so quickly.

ⓑ ... if it's just a little stale, it still can be served up.

ⓒ ... you mean there's an expiration date?

8. The most important thing you learned from gossip is...

ⓐ ... popularity doesn't necessarily last long.

ⓑ ... nerds can be happy people too.

ⓒ ... no one wants to hear old news.

If you answered mostly a's, you're considered a person who understands the shifting, intricate relationships that make some gossip matter more than others. You're close enough to the cool kids to be cool yourself.

If you answered mostly b's, you're close to the middle of things on the gossip ripple effect chart, though not in the center. You like gossip, but you have a ways to go before you become an expert.

If you answered mostly c's, people don't tell you their secrets because they're not safe with you. You love gossip so much, you want to spread it all the time. Hey, this person is the _real_ culprit in the mean e-mail girl rumor — not me! How do I figure out who answered mostly c's? Only a person who answered mostly a's can tell me!

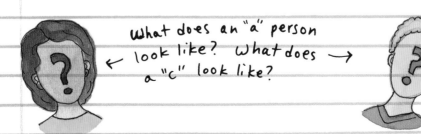

What does an "a" person look like? What does a "c" look like?

I wish I could say I'm in the "a" category, but I'm more in the "b" group. I like gossip (when it's not about me), but I'm not very good at it. To be a grade A gossip, you need to know stuff and you need to know how to tell it in an exciting way. The best gossip in school is Shawna. I wonder if she knows the truth behind the rumor about me.

It's the way she tells you the item — like it's a big secret that only you get to hear, and even though you know she's probably told a million other people, you still feel special. Besides, she only tells quality gossip — the really interesting kind. She leaves the so-so stories to people like me.

You've got to hear the latest about Charisse. This is HOT off the gossip stove!

You know how Max has a crush on Charisse? Well, she knows it too. She sent him an anonymous note telling him that a certain someone likes him the way he likes her.

Of course, that drove Max crazy! He was following Charisse all over the place, hoping to get a chance to talk to her alone. But Charisse just wanted to torment him — she made sure that never happened.

Then, when he was about to give up, she sent him a second note, saying the same thing, only with passion plus!

You can just imagine poor Max! That girl was leading him along by the nose!

Finally, Carly had pity on the poor boy and told him Charisse was just fooling with him. That was the end of that crush — now he hates her! Can you blame him?

Note how she describes a whole dramatic saga, the ups and downs, the pacing of it all — she's a master!

The BIGGEST gossip (not necessarily the best — they're two different things) is Maya. She ALWAYS has a story to share, some juicy, some not-so-juicy, some completely dried-up, but what she lacks in quality, she makes up for in quantity. This can be a good thing <u>and</u> a bad one. If you don't want it spread all over the school, watch what you say to Maya! (And if you want to spread a rumor <u>fast</u>, tell her first.) So maybe <u>she</u> knows who really told on the e-mail girl.

The worst gossip is Leah. Not because she's boring or tells really old, stale stories. Not because she can't tell juicy gossip from a dry shopping list (there are some people like that), but because she always forgets some crucial bit of information. It's so frustrating! Like if she knew who had really told on the girl for sending mean e-mails, she'd forget some major detail – like the kid's name!

There's no point in even asking her about the e-mail rumor.

Wait— was it Lucy this happened to —or Shelly?

Come to think of it, it was a boy. Yes, it was Omar!

So Omar said to Mr. Klein—no, it was Mr. Le Poivre. Anyway, he said to this teacher (whoever it was, I'm not sure), "I can't hand in my homework because my dog ate it." Of course, the teacher didn't believe him and was *very* angry. So he... um... the teacher... give me a second, I'll remember... Oh, wait, you wanted to know about those e-mails, right? That's something else!

Forget about it!

I'm getting a headache on top of my headache!

I'm better than Leah, but I'm a "pass it on" type of gossip. I hear something and I pass it on to my friends. I never get the scoop — the first news of something. And I don't always pass things on. I know when to keep my mouth shut and I'm good at keeping secrets.

At least I'm not a _mean_ gossip — that's a completely different kind of thing. I'm just spreading valuable information. Okay, I admit I've said bad things about Mr. Lambaste — and about Cleo, too — but nothing that wasn't 100% certifiably true. (Okay, maybe the handcuffs weren't true in _fact_, but they were in _spirit_.) I don't spread nasty opinions, only objective facts. It's not my fault if Cleo gets carsick all the time. I don't tell her to chew with her mouth open or sing off-key in a screechy voice. But once she does, I _do_ tell other people about it.

I don't tell personal secrets about her that no one else knows. And I could.

CENSORED

That's my list of private stuff that only someone who lives with Cleo could know about. If I write them down (and I just did), I have to black them out, and I would NEVER say them to anyone. Well, maybe only to Carly because she's my best friend. And I know she's not a gossip. But she told me something GREAT this morning— I'm not being gossiped about anymore! And I didn't even have to get the truth from Shawna or Maya. Instead, the truth came to <u>me</u>.

Here's the story (<u>true</u> gossip, not a false rumor): It was a <u>mom</u> who told the principal about the nasty e-mails. It wasn't even a kid. And yes, it was Shawna who found out the details first.

Some parent was snooping on her kid's computer and found a really ugly message the girl had sent (she even signed her name!). She went right to the principal the next day.

I gave Carly a big hug. "My name's been cleared!" I said.

Carly smiled. "Yeah, you don't have to hide in the library at lunch anymore. But NOW will you admit gossip can be dangerous?"

I know, I know. It's like a bright flame — you can't take your eyes away, but you'd better not get too close.

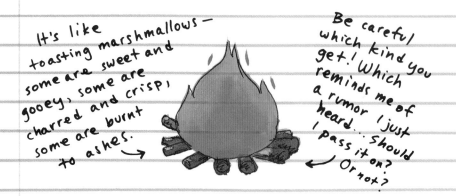

It's like toasting marshmallows — some are sweet and gooey, some are charred and crisp, some are burnt to ashes. →

Be careful which kind you get! Which reminds me of a rumor I just heard... Should I pass it on? ← Or not?

Amelia's Quick Guide to Surviving Middle School Gossip

① Pretend you have <u>no</u> idea there's a horrible rumor about you.

> Have I heard the one about me and the disgusting gym locker?

> Noooo... nope... not a word.

② Act like you know even juicier gossip.

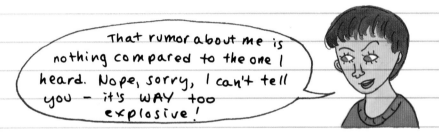

> That rumor about me is nothing compared to the one I heard. Nope, sorry, I can't tell you — it's WAY too explosive!

③ Exaggerate the rumor to make it so ridiculous, it becomes totally unbelievable.

> Yeah, of course I did it!

> Not only did I break into the principal's office, I used my amazing computer skills to change everyone's grades, ages, and last names.

> Wait until it's report card time — what a mess!

This notebook is dedicated to
Sara, Olivia, and Adam
because middle school is coming
sooner than you think!

SIMON & SCHUSTER BOOKS FOR YOUNG READERS
An imprint of Simon & Schuster Children's Publishing Division
1230 Avenue of the Americas, New York, New York 10020

But you
can
share
any
useful
tips!

A Paula Wiseman Book

Thanks,
Tom! →   Book design by Amelia
         (with help from Tom Daly)

you'd
think by →   The text for this book is hand-lettered.
middle   Manufactured in China
school
I'd use a   2 4 6 8 10 9 7 5 3 1
computer — CIP data for this book is available
not me!   from the Library of Congress.

         ISBN-13: 978-1-4169-7987-6